REBEL

M.G. HIGGINS

BREAK AND ENTER

IGGY

ON THE RUN

QWIK CUTTER

REBEL

SCRATCH N' SNITCH

Copyright © 2016 by Saddleback Educational Publishing
All rights reserved. No part of this book may be reproduced in any form or by any means, electronic or mechanical, including photocopying, recording, scanning, or by any information storage and retrieval system, without the written permission of the publisher. SADDLEBACK EDUCATIONAL PUBLISHING and any associated logos are trademarks and/or registered trademarks of Saddleback Educational Publishing.

ISBN-13: 978-1-68021-109-2
ISBN-10: 1-68021-109-9
eBook: 978-1-63078-426-3

Printed in Guangzhou, China
NOR/1015/CA21501554

20 19 18 17 16   1 2 3 4 5

WHITE
LIGHTNING
BOOKS

STATS OF SPORTS IN AFRICA

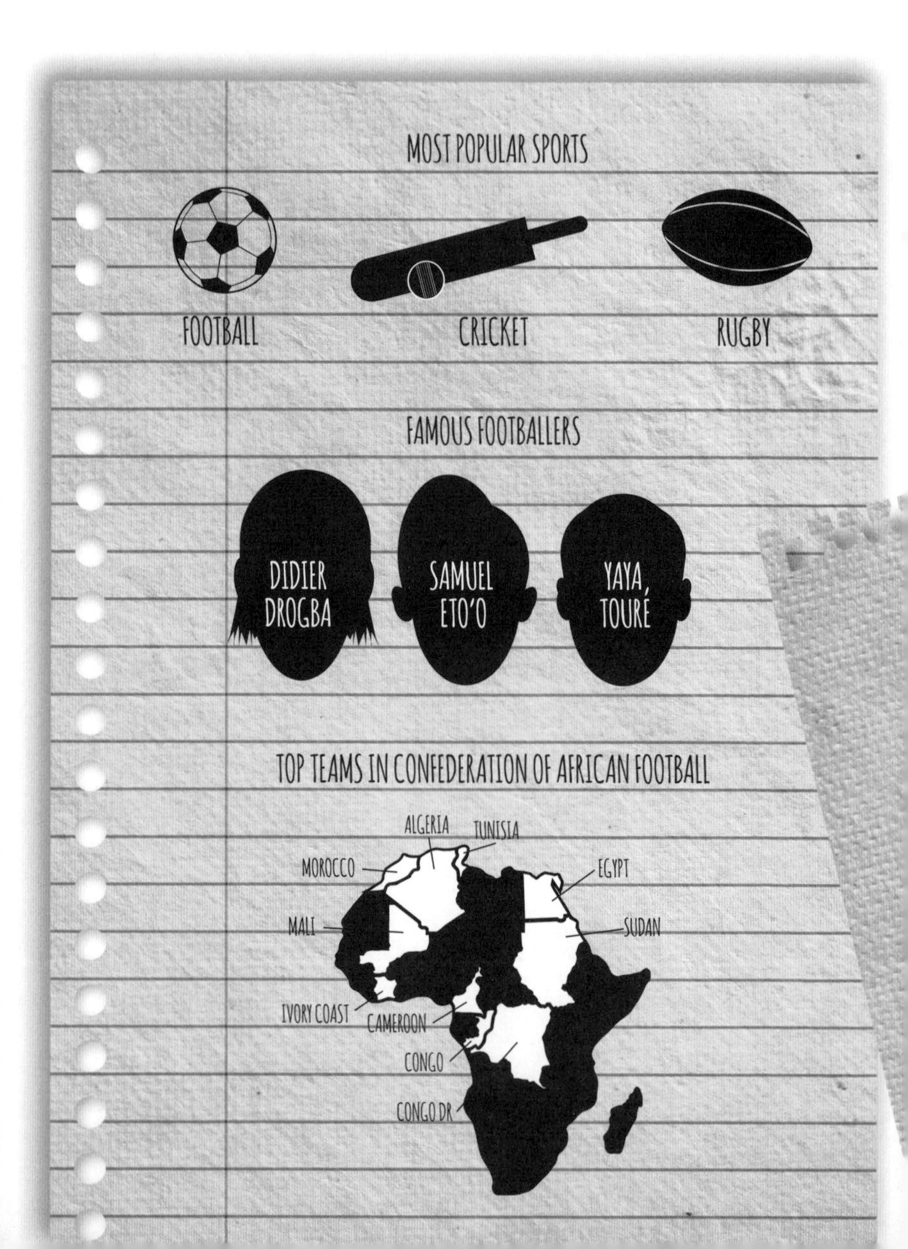

FOOTBALL PASSED DOWN
FROM COUSIN BAAKO

CHAPTER 1

TO SEE THE WORLD

Dear Patrick,

Thank you for your letter. Your family and home in America sound very nice. I would like to visit your country one day. I would especially like to see Disneyland. And I would like to meet Mickey Mouse.

You asked me to describe my home and myself. I live in a small village in Africa. It is the dry season now. It is very dusty. In a few months the rains will come. Then the ground will turn muddy. The grass will grow. I don't like mud. But we need the grass for our cattle.

I have a mother and father. I also have three younger sisters. I have many aunts, uncles, and cousins. Two of my grandparents live in our village. Our house is round. Our roof is made of reeds. The school is square. It has a blue metal roof. It is loud when the rain falls.

My best friend is Jojo. We play soccer. Only we call it football. Do you like football? I like it. I would play it all day long if I could. But I like school too. I like learning about the world. My favorite subject is geography. I want to become a teacher one day.

I am looking forward to being your pen pal.

Sincerely,
Koji

I set my pencil down. Most of my classmates are still writing. Including Jojo. Maybe I should write more. But I read over my letter. Decide it's enough. I hope Patrick writes back. I want to learn more about his life halfway around the world. I pick up my pencil again. Write a note at the bottom of the page.

Please tell me more about your life in America.

There. Now it's enough.

"Time to finish," Mr. Wek says.

Pencils hit the desks.

"Put your letters in the envelopes you addressed," he says. "Pass them to me. I will see that they get mailed."

I watch my letter. It goes hand over hand to the front of the classroom. The beginning of its long journey. I wonder how it will travel. By plane? By boat? I wish I could travel with it.

"Get out your math books," Mr. Wek says.

A few students groan. Jojo too. They don't like math. I don't mind it. I'm going to be a teacher. So I will need to know many things.

It's the end of the day. I'm restless. Want to go outside. But I try to sit still. Don't want a scolding from Mr. Wek. Finally he says, "History exam tomorrow. You may go."

Jojo and I are the first out of our seats. "Race you home," he says.

The village is a mile north. We run the whole way. I sprint at the end. But he still beats me.

"Hah! I won!" he shouts. He throws his hands in the air. Like he's a big champion.

"I'll beat you one of these days," I tell him.

"No you won't," he says. "My legs will always be longer than yours."

"Maybe. But I'm a better footballer."

He laughs. "You are not."

"Am so." I run to our hut. Grab my football. But I don't leave quickly enough.

"Koji!" my mother says. "Change out of your

uniform. And put down that ball. I need you to fetch water."

I groan. "Why can't Onaya do it?"

"Because she's helping me cook. Go on."

I quickly change out of my yellow uniform. I grab the plastic water jug. Carry it outside.

Jojo is playing football with his brothers. I sneak up behind him. Steal the ball out from under his foot. "Hey!" he shouts.

"See?" I laugh. "I told you I'm better!"

I play with them for a few minutes. I'm still holding the water jug. I'm tempted to set it down. And really play. But I need to get going or Mama will be angry.

The pump is at the other end of the village. I pass the village leader's hut. He sits outside. A number of men sit around him. My father's there. I'm surprised to see Papa here. He's usually out with our cattle.

I leave the path. Step closer to them. One man points south. Another points west. They speak in hushed and hurried voices. The one word I hear sends a chill through me. “Soldiers.”

Papa spies me. Shoos me away.

CHAPTER 2

KIDNAPPED

Dinner is quiet that evening. Lines of worry crease Papa's brow. We are all tense. Except for my one-year-old sister. We eat little. Something is wrong. We wait for him to tell us.

"What's going on?" my mother finally asks.

Papa chews slowly. Like he's deciding what to say. "Several of us have seen rebel soldiers while herding. Gamba spied a camp with thirty soldiers."

The icy chill returns to my skin. "What do they want?" I ask.

"Nothing good," he says.

"Tsk," Mama scolds. "You're frightening us."

He nods. "Don't worry. They are probably just passing through. On their way to someplace else."

I try to study for my history exam before bed. But I keep thinking about my father's news. There is a civil war in my country. Rebel soldiers fight against government soldiers. We are just a small village. Not close to any city. The war has not come to us yet. We only hear about it through relatives who live in other places. And from health workers who visit our village. The stories they tell are terrifying. Villages burned. People tortured and killed.

I pray when I go to bed. Go away, soldiers. Do not come here.

I walk with Jojo to school the next day. He also heard about the rebel camp from his father. "We have nothing here that they want," he says. "That's what Papa told us. He said not to worry."

"My father said the same thing," I say.

"Do you believe him?"

I think about it. Papa seemed worried. Even though he told us not to be. "I'm not sure."

I'm suddenly wary of our surroundings. I think I see someone hiding behind a bush. But it is only an antelope. It walks out and runs through the brush. We get to school. Play football in the central yard, like always. But we don't yell or laugh. We whisper about the rebels. We glance around. We slink inside the classroom before the bell rings.

Mr. Wek is the same as ever. He's confident and no-nonsense. Is that because he hasn't heard about the soldiers? Or because he thinks there's no danger? Either way, his calmness helps to calm me. I pay attention to his lessons.

It's late morning. Mr. Wek says, "Time for your history exam. Clear your desks except for a pencil."

I hope I remember enough from his lectures. I did very little studying last night.

The door slams open. Five men burst into the classroom. Point large rifles at us. They are wearing camouflage uniforms.

A boy screams. Another whimpers.

My heart stops.

"All of you stand up!" the tallest soldier barks. He has an ugly scar. It runs across his face. From his forehead, across one eye, down to his chin.

"W-what are you doing here?" Mr. Wek stammers. "What do you want?"

Another soldier moves toward Mr. Wek. He's just a boy. Not much older than me. The fury in his eyes takes my breath away. He bashes the butt of his rifle into our teacher's face. Mr. Wek falls to the floor.

I gasp.

"Stand!" the scar-faced soldier shouts at us. "Now!"

We do as he says. I glance at Jojo. His eyes are wide. Terrified. He doesn't look back at me.

"Leave the room in single file," Scarface commands.

We file out, not daring to disobey.

We're outside. I see that soldiers have emptied all of our school's four classrooms. There are about one hundred students.

It's not cold. But I shiver. Does my father know what's happening? Have the soldiers already been to the village? If so, what did they do? How is my family? I look in that direction. See spirals of dark smoke rise into the air.

A soldier shoves me hard with the side of his rifle. It's the boy who hit Mr. Wek. He glares at me with such hatred. Why? Why does he hate me? "Over there," he snarls. He nods toward a tree. Other boys are also singled out. We huddle together next to the trunk.

I look around. See two other similar groups of students. Each group includes boys of different ages, from ten to sixteen. Jojo stands with a group near the school. He still looks frightened. I'm sure I do too.

The sorting is quickly completed. Now five

soldiers hover around us. Scarface says, "Start walking."

He leads us. I'm in the middle of the line. The other soldiers walk behind and next to us. We march south, away from our village. I glance over my shoulder. Soldiers lead the other two groups in different directions.

The young boy in front of me cries. A bald-headed soldier kicks him. The boy falls to the ground. "Stop crying. If you don't, I'll shoot you."

I go to help the boy up.

"Leave him alone!" the soldier shouts. "Or I will kill you too. Keep going." He jabs the barrel of his rifle hard into my ribs as I walk. "You're a piece of dung," he hisses. "Your family is dung. They are worthless. You are worthless."

I force myself not to cry.

CHAPTER 3

MARCHING

We march without rest. They give us no food. No water. I wonder what happened to the boy who was kicked. I want to look over my shoulder. See if he's at the end of the line. But I don't. I'm afraid what the soldiers will do.

They continue to shower us with insults. Tell us we are worthless pigs. No better than dirt. That we are the children of whores. That they killed our families.

A short, skinny soldier smirks at me. "Your mother. She looks just like you. Small and sweet. Too bad I had to shoot her."

I lower my eyes. Clench my fists. My mother is sweet. I do look like her. People tell me that all the time. Is he telling the truth?

"Do you want to know what happened to your father?" he asks.

I risk a glance at his face. His grin widens. It's an evil grin. Full of hatred. The same hatred they all seem to share.

"He ran like a frightened hare," the soldier says. "I shot him in the back. Along with the rest of your family." He laughs.

Is this true? Is my family dead? I feel a sickness rising in my stomach. I lower my eyes. Press my lips together.

"Do you want to cry?" he asks.

I quickly shake my head.

"Are you thirsty? Hungry?"

I am very thirsty. But I hesitate. Shake my head again.

I feel him stare at me for a long time. Then he walks up the line. He talks to another boy. Is he saying the same things he said to me?

I saw the smoke coming up from my village. I think the soldiers burned our homes. I think I believe him. Does this mean they'll kill me too? Why haven't they done so already? Where are they taking us?

It's dark when we stop marching. They make us sit near some trees. We are shoulder to shoulder. They give us a jug of water. "Only a small amount," the boy soldier says. He watches us closely. One of my classmates sits three boys away. His name is Nuru. He tips the jug back. Keeps drinking.

"Hey!" The boy soldier rips the jug from Nuru's hands. He looks at those of us still waiting. "Because of his greed, you don't get to drink. What do you think I should do to this pig?"

I am so thirsty. More thirsty than I have ever been in my life. I like Nuru. We play football together. But I'm suddenly very angry with him. He got to drink. I didn't. Because he was greedy. But I don't say anything. No one does.

"No ideas?" The boy soldier smirks. "I have a few."

Nuru's eyes widen with fear. He jumps up. It looks like he will run. The boy soldier grabs his arm. Slugs him in the face with his fist. He slugs him again. Nuru falls to the ground. Blood is spurting from his nose. The soldier kicks him in the head. Then in the side. Again. Again. And again.

I close my eyes. Block the sight. I wish I could block my ears from the horrible sound. It is too much. Too much.

Finally the soldier finishes his beating. He walks away. Carries the jug of water.

Nuru lies unmoving in the dirt.

The soldiers make a fire. Start to cook. They sit together, joking and laughing. The smell of cooking food makes my empty stomach hurt. But I don't feel like eating. They eat and drink their fill.

The short, skinny soldier hands us a few nuts. Pieces of dried fruit. Scarface gets to his feet. Walks toward us. I instinctively brace myself for more violence.

"We stand guard at night." He glares at us. "So if you try to run away, we'll shoot. Go to sleep. We march again in the morning."

I curl on the hard ground. I could cry now if I wanted to. They wouldn't see me. But I'm too frightened.

CHAPTER 4

A GLORIOUS LIFE

I awake to the sound of a gun blast. I sit up. My heart is pounding. The rebel soldiers laugh at our shocked and confused expressions.

Nuru sits up slowly. He holds his side. Winces in pain. His face is puffy. One eye is swollen shut. I barely recognize him.

Skinny Soldier gives us a few more nuts. Boy Soldier follows with the water jug. "Not you," he says when the jug gets to Nuru. He pulls it away. Hands it to the next boy.

I finally take my first drink of water. I want to keep drinking. But Boy Soldier is watching. I'm sure he would like any excuse to hurt me. I take two swallows. Pass it along.

I look down our line. Where is the young boy the bald-headed soldier kicked yesterday? I see him at the end. I'm relieved. I wish Jojo were with me. I wonder what he's doing right now. If he's also marching. If he's also in fear for his life.

"Stand!" Scarface shouts.

We all follow his order. Except Nuru. He tries to rise but stumbles to his knees. I want to help him. But I leave him alone. Helping will result in my own punishment. I am sure of it. It angers me that I feel so helpless. It angers me what they're doing to us. Nuru finally stands. Wobbles. Stays on his feet.

"Let's go." Scarface returns to the lead. We follow in a row. Within a few minutes, Nuru staggers. Slows. Those of us behind him stop. Wait.

"Keep going!" Bald Soldier screams. We pass slowly around Nuru. Like he's a rock in our stream. Minutes later a gunshot rings out. It startles a flock of birds from a tree. I want to look behind me to see what happened. But I know. It was Nuru. They killed him. The horror of it makes me want to scream. But I cannot. So I turn off my mind. Try to think of nothing.

We walk all day. It's late in the afternoon. I catch glimpses of more soldiers. We stop under a canopy of trees. There are lots of men here. This must be their camp. Most wear the same camouflage uniforms as our captors. But many—mostly boys—wear regular shorts and shirts. Men and boys alike carry large rifles. So many rifles.

"Sit," Scarface commands us. "Don't move."

I sit on the ground. My body tells me I'm thirsty. And hungry. That my legs are tired. But strangely, I don't care. I gaze at my surroundings. But I don't take anything in.

The water jug returns. I drink two gulps. Pass it on.

They give us more food that night. Not enough to fill me, though. I don't think I'll sleep. Or that I'll ever sleep again. But my mind and body shut down. It does what I'm unwilling to make it do.

"You!" I open my eyes. It's morning. Boy Soldier's hate-filled eyes drill into mine. He pokes the barrel of his rifle into my chest.

I stop breathing. What's wrong? What did I do?

"Get up!" He kicks my leg.

I scramble to my feet.

"Go with him." He gestures with his chin. There's a boy standing a short distance away. I think he's about my age. He's wearing shorts and holding three empty water jugs. "Come right back," Boy Soldier says. "Or we'll find you and kill you."

The boy with the jugs starts walking. I quickly follow him. He waits for me to catch up.

"What's your name?" he asks.

"K-Koji." My heart's beating fast.

"I'm Tuma." He hands me one of the plastic containers. "The pump isn't far. In the closest village. They kicked everyone out. So it's all ours." He eyes my yellow uniform. "They kidnapped you from school?"

I nod. "What about you?"

"I volunteered," Tuma says.

I gape at him. "Volunteered? Why?"

"Why do you think?" He puffs his chest out. "To become a soldier in the rebel army. Fight the government." His chest quickly caves. "For now, I do chores. Fetch water. Firewood. Cook. Clean. Run errands. It's very boring. Not what I expected."

"What did you expect?"

"The images my father put in my head. The glorious life of a soldier. Along with a regular paycheck. I haven't seen either yet." He shrugs his narrow shoulders. "At least there's a little food here. Not something I could always count on at home."

We reach the water pump. It's at the edge of

what should be a village. But all I see are ashy circles where huts should be.

"What happened to the people?" I ask. I wonder again about the fate of my own family.

"Killed or escaped. Don't think about going in there. Still a lot of dead bodies. We're lucky the wind's blowing away from us. The stink is terrible."

My hand shakes as I hold the water jug under the faucet.

CHAPTER 5

RECRUITS

Tuma and I fill our bottles. Walk back to camp.

"They expect us to be soldiers?" I ask. "To kill?"

He looks at me. Like I am very stupid.

"I don't want to be a soldier," I say.

"Then run away. Just make sure they don't catch you. They torture deserters." He looks at me seriously. "Really. Don't try it."

Running away had crossed my mind. Now I'm not sure what to think.

We get back to camp. Set the water bottles on a table. Some boys are preparing food.

"You! Stinking heap of dung!" Bald Soldier shouts at me. "Come here." He's with the other boys from my school. They're removing their uniforms. Pulling shorts and shirts from a pile on the ground. Changing into them. I'm afraid I know where those clothes came from. That destroyed village. I feel sick.

"Hurry up, dung boy!" The soldier points his rifle at me.

I quickly strip off my uniform. Search through the pile of clothes. Find blue shorts. Tug them on. I spy a red sleeveless T-shirt with Soccer written across the front. It reminds me of school. Of Patrick, my new pen pal. He will get my letter. Then write back. But I'll never see his letter. He will never hear from me again. I wanted to learn about America. About the world. I wanted—

A younger boy reaches for the same shirt.

"No!" I shout. I pull it away from him. "It's mine!"

"Says who?"

I slug him in the stomach.

He staggers back. His eyes are wide.

Why did I do that? It was mean. Wrong. But I feel such anger inside me. If he comes for the shirt again, I will hit him. I keep my fist raised to let him know.

I think the boy might whimper or cry. But he returns my angry glare. Goes back to the pile of clothing. Shoves another boy out of his way.

I pull the shirt on. It's too big. But I don't care. It's mine.

I suddenly remember Bald Soldier. Will he punish me for what I just did? I glance at him. He's smiling. As though I just put on a show.

I hate him. I hate all of them.

My schoolmates and I are soon dressed in our new used clothes. Our school uniforms lay in a pile on the ground. Bald Soldier lights them with a match. "Watch your old lives burn away, little dung heaps," he says. He's got a gleeful smile. "At least now your dung-filled lives have purpose."

The fire blazes, heating my face. I was proud of my uniform. Proud of going to school. My life already had purpose. More than he will ever know.

The fire burns low. "Come on," he growls.

We follow him to another area of the camp. There are other boys and young men here. Maybe about fifty. I see Tuma. We sit with them.

Scarface walks up next to Bald Soldier. "This is the area for new recruits," he tells us. He points past the table where we set the water. The area is filled with soldiers in uniform. Most are men. But some are young, including Boy Soldier. They appear relaxed. Talking. Even laughing. "That's where you want to end up," Scarface says. "You will. If you train hard. And we find you worthy."

We are given a small meal that does little to fill my gnawing stomach. I am allowed just enough water to wet my mouth. Then we're told to stand in pairs. They tell us to march. So we do. The sun is hot. A boy falls. A soldier kicks him. A boy vomits. Rolls onto his side. He is shot. I flinch at the sound of the rifle. Will I be next?

We march until sunset. Until I think I will faint. From the lack of water. Food. Sleep. The horror of my new life. But I keep going. It seems I still have the will to live.

CHAPTER 6

TARGET PRACTICE

We return to camp. The sun is setting. Our long march is done. We collapse on the ground. I eat every bite of food they give us. I'm tempted to steal from the boy next to me. But his food disappears inside his mouth as quickly as mine did.

A boy sits on my other side. Tuma. I know from this morning he is the kind of person who likes to talk. But he sits quietly. Stares with vacant eyes at nothing. I wonder if today was his first march. He volunteered. So maybe he hasn't experienced boys being shot. I would like to know what's going through his mind. But I'm too tired to ask. I just want to sleep.

He nudges my arm. Points to the other side of the camp. There, soldiers eat large hot meals. Drink as much as they want. Talk and laugh. I hate them so much. I hate what they're doing to us. "They are devils," I whisper to Tuma.

He nods. "Yes. But that's my goal. I'm going to be there someday. I wonder what it takes."

I don't know. I don't care. I want nothing to do with them. I curl on my side. Don't have enough energy to think about escape.

The next day we march again. Only this time they hand us rifles.

"I know you'd like to kill us," Scarface says with a smirk. "But they're not loaded."

The rifles are big and heavy. There's no ammo. Mine has an arm strap. But I'm not allowed to use it. We march and march. The sun heats the black metal until it is super hot. My arms tire. My hands ache. I hear a gunshot behind me. Did someone drop a rifle? I wonder if that's the punishment. I grip mine tighter.

We return to camp at nightfall. I just want to eat. Drink. Fall asleep. But Boy Soldier is handing out tasks. His brutal eyes land on Tuma and me. "You two. Get firewood." I get to my feet. But tonight I refuse to look away. I don't care if he hits me. Kicks me. Shoots me. I glare at him. Show him all of the hatred he's shown me.

I tense. Prepare for a beating. But he laughs as I walk by. "Whelp of a whore," he spits out. "Make sure you get enough wood."

Tuma and I walk deep into the forest. We collect fallen twigs and branches. I take the opportunity to study my surroundings. Guards are posted everywhere. Perhaps at night I can slip between them. Yes. That is what I'll do. When the timing is right. Running away is my only hope. I will go back to my village. Perhaps that soldier was lying.

Perhaps my family is still alive. Maybe they are looking for me.

My fifth day at the rebel camp begins as usual. It's morning. A bullet is fired from a rifle. That's our wakeup call. We eat almost nothing. Drink almost nothing. I expect to march. But Scarface orders us to a nearby field. It is ringed with armed soldiers. Another soldier passes out rifles.

We sit on the dry grass with our guns. There's a solider I haven't seen before. He explains the parts of the weapon. The magazine, rear sight, front sight, handgrip. He describes how it works. He splits us up into groups of ten. Tuma and I are in the first group.

We lie on our stomachs. Rest our elbows on the ground. Ten targets are nailed to ten wooden posts. Maybe three hundred meters away. The soldier instructs us how to line up the target in the sight. Press the end of the rifle into our shoulders. Squeeze the trigger.

The roar of all those guns is deafening. Tuma laughs with excitement. “This is what I’m talking about!”

I don’t feel excitement. Only dread.

We fire several more rounds. Then we walk down the field. Retrieve our targets.

Tuma and I sit on the ground. Wait for the other groups to finish. We compare our targets. Six of my bullets hit somewhere on the paper. Four within the circles.

“Wow,” Tuma says. “You did better than me. And I bet you weren’t even trying.”

Bald Soldier peers over our shoulders. Looks at our targets. For once, he doesn’t call me dung.

I wonder how soon we’ll be aiming at people instead of paper.

CHAPTER 7

TEST

The camp changes a little that day. Many of the boys are happy to be shooting guns. Others are quiet. I think they know this is not a game. The rebels are training us to go to battle.

The soldiers act as though we've passed a small test. They feed us lunch. It's no more food than they've ever given us. But it's the first midday meal I've had for a week.

Tuma slaps my back. "Good, eh? They're treating us more like them."

I nod in agreement. But is this good? My stomach churns. My hands sweat. I do not want to kill. I do not want to fight for these devils. I need to get out of here. Tonight. I will run away tonight.

A commotion draws our attention. Several soldiers walk into camp. They lead another soldier. His face is beaten and bloody. He staggers. They push him forward. He falls to his knees.

Now what?

Talking and laughter subside. Soldiers stand. Lift their rifles. Scarface talks to one of the man's captors. Then he walks over to us. Points at a boy. "You. Get up." He points at another boy. "You." He meets my eyes. "You." He points at Tuma. "You." He selects eight of us. We stand.

Scarface points at the beaten man. "This soldier tried to run away. He is a deserter. A traitor. Scum. The sentence for desertion is death."

The man's shoulders tremble. He cries. Whimpers, "No. No. No."

A soldier opens a large wooden crate.

"Choose a weapon," Scarface says. "Kill him."

My heart thumps in my chest. I look at Tuma. My fear is reflected on his face. Like a mirror. None of us moves.

"Kill him!" Scarface orders. "Or you will be killed the same way. Kill him. And we may give you more privileges."

Skinny Soldier and Boy Soldier walk toward us. Their rifles are raised.

A boy behind me brushes by my shoulder. He quickly steps to the crate. Selects a curved machete. Slowly, other boys follow his lead. Even Tuma. I am the only one not moving.

I look at the crying man. He tried to run away. The same thing I'd planned to do tonight. He is an adult. He knows these people. He knew what he was doing. I am a child, who knows nothing. It hits me like a kick to my stomach. A deluge of rain. There is no hope. I am trapped here. I cannot get away. Either I kill, or I will be killed.

I glare at Scarface. He looks back at me with

a twisted, vicious smile. I hate that they took me. Hate that they killed my family. Hate that they starve me. Insult me. Threaten me.

Hate. Anger.

It fills me. It is all I see. All I feel.

I march to the box. Grab the closest weapon. It's a long double-edged knife.

By now the captured soldier lies on the ground. He's bleeding from the small wounds he's receiving. He cries and flails. Tries to protect himself with his arms and hands. But I no longer see a man. I see a pile of simpering flesh. He sickens me. I want this to end.

I kneel above his head. Slice my knife deep across his throat.

He stops moving. Blood from my cut seeps onto the ground. Pools under his shoulders and head.

A cheer goes up. Soldiers shoot bullets into the sky.

That night they move me to the other side of the camp.

They give me a full meal.

They give me a uniform.

CHAPTER 8

PROMOTED

The other boys also did what they were told. They attacked the deserter. But I am the only one promoted that day. It's the next morning. Boy Soldier explains it to me. I slowly eat breakfast. My stomach has shrunk. It twists in a knot. It's hard to get everything down.

"I was the same as you," he says. "Kidnapped from my village. Ordered to kill someone. In my case, it was a woman they captured. I didn't want to. She reminded me of my mother. But I decided right away I wanted to be a solider." He looks over at me. "Landing the deadly blow is good. It shows you're a killer. I did the same thing. Only I shoved my knife into her heart." He sets his plate on the ground. "They don't tell you beforehand. But whoever does the actual killing is promoted." He shrugs. "Plus, I hear your shooting is pretty good."

That day I am given my own rifle. I practice more shooting. Learn how to clean the gun. Scarface sits next to me. I'm putting the rifle back together. I have learned the other men call him Alpha. It stands for leader. For once he doesn't glare at me. I'm not a cockroach about to be squashed under his boot.

"Do you know why we fight?" he asks.

I shake my head.

"To overthrow the corrupt government. They are a sham. The president took power illegally. We are fighting for your tribe. For my tribe." He pounds his fist against his chest. Then he sticks his fist in front of him. I bump it with mine because

I think that's what he wants. Before leaving, he smiles kindly. Slaps my shoulder.

A week goes by. I train and march. I don't have to fetch water. Don't have to fetch firewood. No cooking or cleaning either. The boys on the other side of the camp do those chores. Soldiers no longer stare at me like I'm worthless. I learn their names. Boy Soldier calls himself AK. It stands for AK-47. Those are rifles we use. He gives me the nickname Slice. It's for the way I killed the deserter. At least it gets more respect than Dung Heap.

I overhear soldiers talking about an upcoming battle. It will take place near the capital. That's over ninety miles away. Before we leave, thirty boys are promoted. Given uniforms and rifles. One of the new soldiers is Tuma. He joins me after changing clothes. His uniform hangs loose on his bony frame.

"Finally," he says. "Food and a paycheck. I wish I knew what would have happened. Because I'd have killed that deserter myself."

I don't say anything. There is a difference between us now. I looked up to Tuma when I first arrived at camp. He seemed to know so much more than me. Now he looks up to me. And I see the respect in his eyes. Even some fear. I'm one of the rebels. My name is Slice. Alpha, the leader, has taken a liking to me.

It is not a terrible feeling. Being in power is much better than being picked on.

We train as a unit for two days. Then we march. There are one hundred of us all together. And some boys who will cook. Help with chores. It will take a long time to reach our destination. But we're in shape after so much training.

It's the third day of marching. We come to a village. Alpha stops us at the edge. "Burn it to the ground," he orders. "Kill everyone you find." We file past him. He watches us closely.

I try to keep my expression neutral. I don't want him to question my loyalty. I have killed a soldier. And I will kill the enemy when the time comes. But this doesn't feel right. What have these villagers done to us? Are they our enemy?

I look over at AK. He's walking next to me. His expression is flat. Uncaring. He's done this before.

"Why?" I whisper.

He shrugs. "To frighten people into submission. To show the government we mean business. And because you need training."

"What? I don't understand."

"Most of the new soldiers haven't killed yet," he says. "Alpha will be watching. Don't mess this up." Moments later he rushes into the village. His rifle is raised. He shoots at children, women, old people. Anything that moves.

CHAPTER 9

BATTLE

A sickening dread churns in my gut. This is not what I want. I did not ask for this.

But I have no choice. If I refuse? They will kill me. If I run? They will kill me. I must do what I'm told. Plus, I've gained Alpha's respect. I don't want to lose it.

I step into the village. One of our soldiers lights a hut on fire. A woman runs out with a child. She's holding his hand. I raise my rifle. She sees me. Stops. Pushes her son behind her back. Guards him. I hesitate. Then I remember the soldier whose throat I slit. This woman is only a pile of flesh like him. I pull the trigger. She goes down. I quickly shoot the child.

"No! You devil!" a man cries.

I twist around. He comes at me with a knife. He's screaming. I shoot him in the chest.

There are so many of us. And the villagers are poorly armed. It is over quickly. A massacre. I walk around the village. Look for movement. Maybe there's someone else to shoot. But I see only bodies. Burning huts. A few shots ring out. Soldiers have found people trying to escape.

We gather food from the village. Anything of value.

Then we make camp a few miles away.

Tuma sits with me while we eat. The rations have been small on this march. But tonight we eat meat and vegetables we stole from the village. We are both quiet. I don't want to think about what happened. And yet it doesn't bother me as much as it should. I should care. I should weep for those people. Especially the women and children. But I cannot muster sympathy. Perhaps because I have none to give.

That night Alpha sits before us on a tree stump. He tells us stories of the rebellion. Of the evil people in power. The need to get rid of them. Some soldiers cheer with excitement. They are true believers. The rest of us also cheer. But only because it is expected of us.

Two days later we arrive near the capital. Other units of rebel soldiers have joined us. I see classmates from my village school. But not Jojo. Is he alive? I don't have much time to wonder about him. The battle soon begins. We fight the government forces in a slum just outside the city.

Firing at soldiers is easy. Much easier than killing villagers. I fight with great energy. With hateful enthusiasm. With little fear. I shoot and shoot. I hide behind trash bins. Buildings. Old cars.

I don't know how many people I kill or injure. I lose count.

Eventually we retreat several miles away to a makeshift camp. I am tired, but my body vibrates with nervous energy. Tuma survived. And AK. I learn that the man I used to call Bald Soldier died. Many others from our unit died too.

We fight again the next day. Then Alpha leads us away. To the southeast. Away from our original training camp.

"We are gnats swarming in the government's face," he tells us that night. "We are leeches burrowing into their skin." Then he shouts, "We are rebel soldiers!" He fires his rifle into the sky. We shout and do the same.

Then Alpha explains the war is not over. There will be more skirmishes. More battles. But our ranks have thinned. He looks at me when he asks for volunteers to recruit new soldiers.

I raise my rifle.

He smiles and nods.

CHAPTER 10

VOLUNTEER

I am not familiar with this part of the country. It is wetter here than where I'm from. More green. More hills. And the rainy season has begun. Our feet drag through mud. Water drips down our heads.

There are twelve of us. Tuma is with me. And AK. So is Mosi. I used to call him Skinny Soldier. He leads us. Alpha leads a different recruiting mission. We wait in the brush until dark.

School is not in session. So we'll have to raid a village. It's not as easy as a school, Mosi tells us. But it's easy enough. He assigns two soldiers to stay nearby to guard the recruits. "We'll go to each hut in pairs," he says. "Take any boy between the ages of ten and sixteen. If an adult resists, kill them. But use your knives, not rifles. As soon as the villagers realize what's happening, they will run and hide."

I go with AK. Tuma goes with Mosi. With ten soldiers, we'll be able to clear five huts at a time. AK and I take the third hut. We go inside. A woman screams. "Shut up," AK orders her. She screams again. I hit her with the butt of my rifle. She falls.

A man reaches toward a table. I spy a chopping knife. "Don't," I yell. "Or I'll kill all of you."

He stops. His face is frozen in fear and disbelief. I am only a child. But I terrify him.

There are five children in the hut. Two girls, three boys. Two of the boys are the right age. Maybe around eleven and thirteen. The other is too young.

"You and you." AK gestures at the two boys with his rifle. "Come with us."

"No," the father pleads. "Don't take them. They are just boys. We're farmers, not soldiers." He holds his arm out to block them from leaving.

I pull out my knife. Shove it against his chest. He slowly lowers his arm. The boys stand there. "Little swine," I hiss at them. "Do you want me to kill your father?"

The older boy shakes his head.

"Then hurry up!"

He grabs his brother's hand. They leave the hut. We deliver them to the soldiers standing guard.

There are no boys in the next hut. One in the following. We take him easily.

It is quickly over.

We march fifteen boys in single file through the rain and the mud. A boy slips. I kick him. "Get up, you piece of dung." He scrambles to his feet. He looks up at me with fear. Loathing. He hates me. The same way I hated AK. The same way I hated all of them. And it hits me in that moment. This is how it begins. This is how rebel soldiers are made.

We march them most of the night. We camp for a few hours. Give them a little food. A little water. A little rest. Just enough to keep them going.

We punish them enough to fear us. Taunt them enough to lose hope.

Then when they despise us enough. When they're filled with enough rage at what we've done to them. They will want to be one of us. To do to others what we've done to them. They will want to kill.

I see it so clearly now. So clearly I think something will shift. That the thing inside me the rebels have broken will fix itself.

The next morning Mosi wakes the boys with a gunshot. I laugh at their confused and frightened expressions. I pass the jug of water. Watch carefully. Make sure they take only a few sips. If not, I slug them or kick them.

We march them the entire day. Now that Bald Soldier has died, I take his place calling boys dung. Heaps of dung. Smelly dung. Dung face.

No. I am too far-gone to ever be Koji again. My hatred is too great. My anger is too much. I cannot be fixed.

CHAPTER 11

DECISION

We march our boys to a new training camp. The other teams arrive with more recruits. Now we have forty-five boys to train. It is the same for them as it was for Tuma and me. Marching to exhaustion. Hunger. Thirst. Beatings. Bullying. Only now I am the one who bullies and beats.

We give them little rest. The boys send angry and envious glances to our side of the camp. None of them realizes that's how it's supposed to be. We want them angry. Envious. It means we are doing our jobs.

Thirty-six of the boys survive training. Become soldiers. We go on more missions. Kill more civilians. More government soldiers.

We march north. The terrain becomes familiar. Drier, flatter. Then I begin to recognize landmarks. Jackal Hill. Elephant Rock. My heart speeds up. This is home.

We pass a vacant school. My old school. It should be full of students. But the doors hang open. Weeds and junk fill the central yard. That's where I used to play soccer with Jojo and my classmates. I remember Mr. Wek. I remember before I was kidnapped. We had just begun writing to pen pals. My pen pal was Patrick. He lived in the U.S.

My favorite subject was geography. I wanted to learn about the world. I wanted to be a teacher.

We keep marching down the path that passes my old village. My heart races. Is anyone from my family still there? Mama? Papa? My sisters? Are they alive?

I have been in the rebel army for eight months. I have not thought about my family or school for a very long time. Thinking about my old life brings sadness. Hopelessness. Deep shame for the things I have done. We march past my village. And I can't help thinking about my life. How disappointed my mother would be with me. My father too. In a way, I hope they are dead. So they will never learn what I've become.

Most of the huts are gone. I see no people, only a stray dog.

"Hey," Tuma says, marching next to me. "Hurry up."

I walk faster. Focus my eyes front. I don't want to see more of my destroyed village. Don't want to remember.

We march another mile. Make camp for the night. These are the fields where my father grazed our cattle. There are no cattle now.

I try to eat. But my stomach clenches. My mind keeps going home. I think about what I have lost. What I miss. What I could have been if the rebels had not taken me.

Tuma nudges my arm. Looks at my food. “Are you going to eat that?”

I shake my head.

He takes it. “What’s wrong? You never leave food uneaten.”

The knot in my stomach tightens. The tight feeling moves into my chest. Crawls down my arms and legs. I feel as though I can’t move.

“Koji?” Tuma says. He must be worried. He’s using my real name instead of Slice.

I somehow make my mouth work. “That was my village we passed,” I say softly. “That was my school. I used to play football. I wanted to be a teacher.” Tears come. I don’t want them to. I order them to stop. But they don’t obey.

I lower my eyes so no one sees. Rebel soldiers don’t cry. But why shouldn’t I cry? I’m still only twelve. I've lost my entire family. All of my friends. My future. I am a murderer. And it's because of them. Alpha. The others. Hate and anger rise to the surface.

I curl my fingers into fists. Look over at Tuma. Should I tell him what I'm thinking? Can I trust him?

His eyes widen at the sight of my tears. "What's going on?" he asks.

"Do you ever think about running away?" I whisper.

CHAPTER 12

A PLAN

Tuma shrinks away from me. We both know what Alpha does to deserters. Not just death. But a slow, horrible death. He stares at the ground for a long time. I did the wrong thing. He's a professional soldier. He volunteered to be here. He's going to report me to Alpha. I'll be killed for even considering it.

I break out in a sweat. "Never mind," I say quickly. "I didn't mean it. I was just feeling sorry for myself."

He leans in. Whispers low. I barely hear him. "I think about it all the time. I'm sick of marching. Sick of fighting."

"What about your father?" I ask. "Won't he be angry if you return home?"

He pauses. "I'm not going back to that slum. I want to go to school. Get a job."

I take a deep breath. "So how do we do it?"

"I don't know. I don't know if it's possible."

I think. "Soldiers disappear all the time. We're told they were killed in battle. But do we know for sure?"

"No," Tuma says. "We don't."

As a rebel soldier, I only consider the next moment. My next task. My next meal. My next battle. Now I look further into the future. Escape. How we will do it. Where we will go. It gives me some hope. And it fills me with terror.

Tuma and I talk about it whenever we're alone. We come up with ideas. Decide why they won't work. Come up with new ideas. We listen to Alpha's conversations with other leaders. Try to learn where we're going. And when.

We finally agree on a plan. It will be dangerous. It will require perfect timing.

Alpha marches us north. We join another unit of soldiers. We're at the wooded camp where we originally trained. Trying to escape from here frightens me. It's where the deserter was caught. The soldier we had to kill. But we need trees to make our plan work.

There are no recruits in training right now. And we are a large group. Soldiers—especially boys like us—are enlisted to help with chores. Tuma and I gladly accept all assignments.

We do an especially good job finding firewood. We bring back large armloads. We hope to be sent out on this task often. The first time we go, I shove a piece of rope up my shirt. We find a distinctive tree. A large branch has broken off. It leaves a scar in the shape of a face.

We dig a hole at the base of the trunk. Bury

the rope. We bury another piece of rope on our next trip. Two knives on the trip after that. Then plastic bottles filled with water. Shorts and shirts. A shoulder bag. We save dried fruit and nuts from our meals. Wrap them to keep the rodents away. We bury them too.

It is the second week we've been in camp. Alpha makes an announcement after our evening meal. "We march to a new battle the day after tomorrow. We will bury the government pigs! We will take back our country!"

Tuma and I shout our excitement. So does everyone else. We raise our rifles. Fire bullets into the sky.

We lie down to sleep that night. "It must be tomorrow," I whisper.

"Tomorrow," Tuma agrees.

I sleep little, tossing and turning.

The following morning we gather firewood for breakfast. We return with more than usual. We gather firewood for lunch. Still more than usual. We hope the cooks will have enough to start the evening meal. Then nobody will miss us right away.

We leave to gather firewood for dinner. We walk quickly. But not so quickly we'll raise suspicion. As always, guards surround the camp. They're used to us. They know we have to travel far to collect wood. That we need to take different routes. We reach the last perimeter guard. It's Vanu.

"Hey," Vanu says. "What's for dinner?"

"What do you think, idiot?" Tuma says. "Same as last night."

"Bastard." Vanu laughs. He makes a rude gesture.

We're out of his sight. We rush to our secret tree. Quickly unearth our supplies. Change out of our uniforms and into the shorts and shirts. We bury the uniforms in the same hole. Cover it completely with dirt and leaves.

We each take a knife. Tie the sections of rope

around our waists. I shove the food and water into the bag. Loop it over my shoulder.

I glance at Tuma.

He nods.

We run.

CHAPTER 13

ESCAPE

Tuma and I race through the trees.

"How much time until they miss us?" I wonder aloud.

"Another hour, I think. Hopefully longer."

Earlier, he explained that he came this way when he joined the rebels. The forest stretches several miles. It ends in grassland. We want to stay in the forest as long as we can.

The sun lowers. It will set soon. We slow to a walk. Look for a tree.

"There," Tuma says. He points to a tall tree with many limbs. It looks sturdy. It has a thick canopy of leaves. He shimmies up the trunk. Grips it with his legs. He reaches the first large limb. "Come on," he calls. "Hurry."

I scurry up. Scrape my bare arms and legs on the rough bark. From the first limb, we pull ourselves up, branch by branch. Until the limbs become too thin to hold us. "We can't go higher," I say.

"But I can still see the ground through the leaves," Tuma says nervously. "They can spot us."

"We can't help that. We don't have time to find another."

I straddle the limb I'm on. Untie the rope from my waist. Lash myself to the trunk.

Tuma chooses a limb on the other side of the trunk, just above me. I hear him tying himself in the same way.

It's almost dark. I'm hungry. Thirsty. I pull the bag around to open it. That's when I hear shouting. I freeze. Hold my breath.

Leaves crunch nearby. Someone shouts from farther away. It sounds as though they're spread out. Probably searching for us. I lean over. Look down. A soldier stands just underneath our tree. He scans this way and that. Gazes into the forest. I quickly straighten. Press the back of my head against the trunk. Don't look up, I pray. Please don't look up.

I imagine receiving a hundred knife wounds. Wonder how long it will take to die. I start to shiver. The bag slips. I grab it.

Leaves crunch again. Did he hear me? Is he looking up? Does he see me?

I freeze. Prepare myself for a gunshot to my foot or leg.

But it doesn't come.

It's hard to say how much time passes. Minutes? Hours?

After a while, the silence is complete. I wait longer. Finally take a full breath. "Tuma?" I whisper.

"Yes." His voice shakes.

I pull a water bottle from the bag. Hand it up to him.

It's not easy sleeping while tied to a tree. Not knowing when the soldiers will return. I think I manage an hour or two.

We climb down before dawn.

"Do you think they're still out here?" I whisper. "Or did they return to camp?"

Tuma shrugs. "They're supposed to start for that battle today."

"Except Alpha hates deserters. I think he might leave men behind. So he can make examples of us."

We walk quietly. Swiftly. All the time listening for noises in the brush.

It's early afternoon. We reach the edge of the woods. Our only path now goes across the grasslands. In the open. We stop and stare at the vast expanse.

I know Tuma is thinking the same thing. We will be easy targets for anyone with a rifle.

"Maybe we should find another tree," I suggest. "Try to sleep. Then head out at night."

He doesn't argue.

The trees here are not very large. But we find the one with the most limbs and leaves. We climb up. Tie ourselves in. Eat little. Drink little. We're unsure how long our water and food will last. How long will it take to finally escape?

I'm so used to gunfire. So the shot almost doesn't wake me. But then I remember that Tuma and I are up a tree. We're hiding from rebel soldiers who want to kill us. I become very alert, my skin tingling. The shot was close. But it didn't hit nearby. I don't think it was meant for us.

Who is firing? Why?

CHAPTER 14

THE ROAD

The single rifle shot becomes many shots. They resound through the forest.

I catch sight of a man in uniform. He's passing under our tree. Not a rebel. A government soldier. Are they fighting the rebels Alpha sent to capture us?

My mind carries out a battle of its own. I have no love of government soldiers. They have tried to kill me many times. They are the enemy. Part of me wants to climb down this tree. Join my comrades. Shoot as many of them as I can.

But the rebels will kill me. Just like the government soldiers will kill me. And my former "comrades" will beat and torture me first.

So I stay where I am. Let the rebels fight for their lives. They are not looking for us.

Gradually the shots quiet. The skirmish moves deeper into the forest.

"Should we go or stay?" I ask Tuma.

He's silent a long moment. "Maybe we should wait until nightfall."

I look at the horizon. It will be dark in an hour. "Either side may come back after their battle is finished. At least now we have a little light to see by."

I hear him untying his rope. He must agree with me.

We scurry down the tree. Take one last cautious look. Then we leave the safety of the forest. Seeing no soldiers, we run through the grass. Is there a target on my back? It feels like it.

We run until it is too dark to see. Then we walk.

I may hate government soldiers. But we're in an area under their control. And it's safer than where we were. We look like village boys without our uniforms. They shouldn't recognize us. I search through the bag. Look for anything that might connect us to our recent lives. Only the knives could give us away. I don't want to get rid of mine. I doubt Tuma does either.

"What should we say if someone asks about our knives?" I ask.

He thinks. "We got them off dead rebel soldiers."

I nod. "We can say we're friends from the south. That our village was attacked. We were playing ball. We ran and hid."

We don't need the ropes anymore. They may lead to questions. I untie mine from my waist. Throw it into the grass. Tuma does the same.

We walk quietly most of the night. I don't know this area. But Tuma assures me there is a road up ahead.

We're too hungry and tired to keep going.

We sleep on the ground for a few hours. Then we wake at first light. We eat the last of the nuts and dried fruit. I take a swallow of water. Tuma tilts the bottle back. Finishes it. We don't have to say what we both know. Getting caught by soldiers is no longer our biggest problem. We must find water and food soon. We won't survive otherwise.

A few hours later, we see a road. It is filled with people. The only vehicles appear to be government jeeps and trucks.

We reach the road. Blend in with the crowd. A boy my age walks behind a woman holding an infant. I step up next to him. "Where are you going?" I ask.

He eyes me. Like I should know.

"We have just arrived," I explain. "Our village was attacked."

"We're going to a refugee camp," he says softly.

"Do you have water?" I ask.

He quickly shakes his head.

He's lying. I know it. Anger simmers. Doesn't

he know who I am? I could so easily stab him. Kill him and his family. Take everything they own.

Tuma must see the lightning in my eyes. He grabs my arm. Pulls me back. "Don't be stupid."

"But we need water," I say.

He lets me go. Stops and speaks to an elderly man behind us. Returns a moment later. "The camp is about five miles away. We'll last that long without water."

I suppose we will. And we've escaped from the rebels. It should make me feel relieved. Joyful. Yet my anger remains. My past has come with me. And it is filled with hate.

CHAPTER 15

REFUGEE CAMP

We reach the top of a small hill. White shapes dot the valley below. Domed tents. Hundreds of them. And people. So many people.

We walk with the crowd of refugees. Men in blue caps begin appearing. They are holding rifles. Their blue vests say UN. They tell us we must register. They direct us to stand in a long line. The line snakes to a large white canopy. I don't want to wait. I don't want to register.

What will they do if they find out we were rebel soldiers?

"I don't like this," I tell Tuma. "I want to leave."

"We need food and water," he says. "And anywhere we go we risk running into rebels. They'll recognize us. Kills us."

He's right. I hate that he's right.

A woman wearing a blue UN hat and vest hands out bottles of water. I drink mine greedily.

It takes more than an hour. But we finally reach the large canopy. A man directs me to an empty table. The woman at the table asks me questions. My name. Age. Village. I answer honestly.

Then she asks, "How did you end up here?"

I hesitate. "I escaped when my village was attacked."

"That village was attacked nine months ago," she says.

I lower my eyes. "I've been running. And hiding."

"For nine months?"

I don't answer.

"Were you a rebel soldier?" she asks. "We know they kidnapped boys from your school."

I shake my head.

"It's okay," she says softly. "You're safe now."

I don't believe her. I move to get up. Run away.

"Koji, wait," she says. "Please, stay. There are other boys here like you. There are people who can help."

I slowly look at her.

"I assure you, you are safe," she repeats. "You can be a boy again. Isn't that what you want?"

Tears come to my eyes. "I don't know how to be a boy anymore."

She nods. "I understand. Let me see if any of your family is here."

She is wasting her time. After what I have seen and done, I know my family must be dead. But I settle back in the chair. She reads through pages of long lists.

She presses her finger on the third page. Looks up. "Your mother and a sister."

My eyes widen. "They're here? Are you sure?"

"I will add your name to their tent. This gentleman will take you." She gestures to a man with a blue cap.

"But my friend, Tuma." I stand. Look around the large room. Don't see him.

"You can find him later," the woman says. By now another refugee is already taking my empty seat.

I follow the man down row after row of domed white tents. They are set close together. Adults and children crowd the small lanes. It stinks of human waste.

"Here." The man points at a tent and leaves.

I pull the flap aside. "Mama?"

It is dark inside. My eyes slowly adjust. My mother sits on a mat. She's holding my baby sister, Nala. Lines crease Mama's face. She looks like an old woman. She gazes at me. It's like she's seeing a ghost. She gasps. Sets Nala down. "Koji." Then we are in each other's arms. She cries like she will never stop.

Later, I ask her what happened to the village. To our family.

"Lookouts watched the rebel camp." She stares blankly across the narrow room. "They warned us just before the rebels attacked. I scooped up Nala. I thought …" She starts to cry. "I thought Onaya and Mali were right behind me."

"They didn't make it? Or Papa?" I ask.

She shakes her head. Buries her face in her hands. Later, she says UN officials told her rebels kidnapped students from my school. She doesn't ask what my life was like as a soldier. I will never tell her.

I spend the next few days glancing over my shoulder. Afraid of every sound, every movement. I'm certain rebel soldiers are about to capture me. I wake up from nightmares. Of running and hiding. Alpha's scarred face. Death. Hunger. Fear.

Mama cooks. It is good to eat her food again.

To feel cared for. But I am no longer her little boy. I don't know what I am.

I spend the first days wandering through the camp. I find Tuma. His uncle and three cousins are here. He lives with them. I look for my old friend Jojo. But I can't find him. Or any members of his family. I wonder if he is alive. If I will ever see him again.

Tuma and I talk about what happens next. This is not a good place. It is crowded. Dirty. There is no school. No work. But we can't leave the refugee camp. Rebel soldiers will likely capture us. Or government soldiers might try to recruit us into their army. And where would I go? My village no longer exists. So we are stuck here. Maybe until the war ends. No one knows when that will be.

At least I am alive.

"Koji!" Tuma shouts. "Over here." He holds up his hand. I kick him the ball. Dust blows around our bare feet. We run to the goal.

It is my sixth month in the refugee camp.

There are many makeshift football fields like this one. I prefer to play with Tuma. And with the other boys like us. Boys who were soldiers. There are more than twenty of us. It didn't take long for Tuma and me to find them. Then they led us to the aides. They help former soldiers. The aides talk to us. Give us advice. I believe them. Because they were once soldiers too.

The ball comes toward me. Another boy and I chase it. I catch it under my foot. He tries to steal it from me. I shove him hard with my elbow. He shoves me back. Soon we are fighting. I punch him in the face. My anger is always close to the surface. He punches me back. His rage is equal to mine.

Kids pull us apart. "Breathe," Tuma orders me.

At first I don't hear him. I see only red. Struggle to get away.

Tuma shakes me. "Breathe!"

It's what the aides tell us all the time. A way to deal with our anger.

Finally I hear Tuma. I breathe. Push him away. Go to the sideline. Try to calm down.

The boy I hit does the same thing. In the moment we were fighting we hated each other. But now I nod at him. He nods back. That's why I only play with these boys. We understand each other.

The aides say it will take a long time to work through the hate, rage, and shame. Maybe many years. The boy I was is gone. One day I may find him again. But by then I'll be a man.

In the meantime I breathe. Tell myself I was forced to be a soldier. I would not have done any of those things on my own.

"Koji, come on!" Tuma waves me back into the game.

I run in. Play as hard as I can. Cling to these moments of boyhood on the field.

WANT TO KEEP READING?

9781680211054

Turn the page for a sneak peek at another book in the White Lightning series:

ON THE RUN

CHAPTER 1

TRACK STAR

The sun was shining. A cool breeze blew.

Great weather for running, Jack Porter thought.

Jack was standing at his high school track. All around him runners stretched. They warmed up.

Small tents circled the track. High school banners flew in front of each one. The smell of hot dogs and hamburgers filled the air.

"Testing," said a voice over the loudspeaker. "One, two, three."

The biggest track meet of the season was about to start. Schools from across the state had come to East Lake High. East Lake was Jack's home track. West Lake, the school across town, was there too.

The biggest contests were always between the two schools. Everyone at West wanted to beat East. And everyone at East wanted to beat West.

Jack didn't care about beating West. He cared about beating everyone. For him, this meet was extra important. He was a senior. These would be his last home races. And he wanted to go out a winner.

"Good luck, Jack," one runner said.

Jack nodded. "You too."

"We're rooting for you," said another.

Jack just smiled.

Those guys went to another school. Jack didn't know them. But everyone knew Jack.

Jack Porter was a star. Pretty amazing, he knew. Years ago, no one paid attention to him. Or if they did? They teased him. Kids even bullied him sometimes. Jack used to be a skinny kid. Funny-looking. Back then he just didn't fit in.

In high school Jack wanted things to change. So he joined clubs. He worked on the school newspaper. That helped a bit. He made one friend: a boy named Luke. Luke didn't fit in either. They spent time together. They hung out. But it wasn't enough.

Jack wasn't an athlete. He knew that. But he always loved to run. So he tried out for track. And he found his place. He grew taller and stronger. His straight brown hair turned gold in the sun.

Jack looked different. And he acted different too. For the first time, he felt sure of himself.

Soon, Jack was the number one runner. He made a ton of friends. It became hard for Jack to remember the past. How it was before. How he felt out of place. How he wanted people to like him.

But that was then. This was now.

"Runners! Check in for the mile," the announcer said.

Jack slipped on his spikes. He tied the laces tight. He did one more stretch. Then he stood up straight. He had a race to win.